Baby For The Serp General

Alien Baby Pact, Volume 7

Aurelia Skye and Juno Wells

Published by Amourisa Press, 2023.

JOIN JUNO WELLS' NEW RELEASE LIST!

Click on this link (or copy and paste it into your browser):

http://eepurl.com/bnMJL5

Join Kit's Mailing List[1] **(www.kittunstall.com/newsletter) to receive notification of new releases and access bonus chapters for your favorite books. You get free books just for signing up. If you prefer to receive notifications for just one, or a few, of Kit's pen names, you'll have the option to select which lists to subscribe to at signup.**

---

1. http://kittunstall.com/newsletter/

Blurb

She's his reluctant captive, but can she become his willing mate? CAPTURED REBEL NATALIA expects to be executed, not claimed as a surrogate by General Zath, a fierce Serpentine alien. While wary, she's intrigued by his unexpected care and eventual admission he desires her as a true mate. Torn between lingering distrust and her growing feelings, Natalia must decide if she can abandon her cause to find love in the enemy's arms.

Seven years ago, the Faction agreed to save Earth from the vorathan invasion in exchange for Earth women giving them one year of proxy rights to act as a surrogate, since the aliens of the Faction faced a dwindling population. With the vorathans feared throughout the galaxy as bloodthirsty, vicious marauders, the Earth's government agreed.

That doesn't mean the women did.

Sometimes, you want to read about the entire alien empire and all its myriad twists and turns, immersing yourself in hundreds of pages of intrigue. And sometimes, you want to skip the frills and get to the main event. Juno and Aurelia are pleased to bring you a series of short, steamy romances about human women making babies with their truly alien mates.

Chapter One

NATALIA PACED THE SMALL confines of her cell, frustration and anger churning within her. She had no idea how long she'd been imprisoned in the depths of the Faction Embassy. There were no windows or clocks, and nothing to mark the endless passage of time. Just the four blank walls of her cell and the forcefield across the entrance. A tiny window deactivated twice per day to allow a guard to deliver her meals.

She was filthy, having been given no means to wash herself or her tattered clothing aside from the small sink beside the commode. Her formerly blonde hair must be nearly black by now. Not that she cared much about her appearance anymore. Not when her fate was so uncertain.

She had expected execution after the failed rescue/abduction of Rana. What else could she expect as a member of the human rebellion against the Faction proxy agreement? Yet hours had turned into days with no sign that her death was imminent.

The not knowing was the worst torture. The isolation. The boredom. The questions with no answers. Why had they not killed her yet? For what were they waiting? Natalia could only assume they intended to make an example of her, perhaps filming her execution for propaganda purposes. A public execution would send a clear message to others who might dissent. Humans had to accept their place, bowing meekly to serve as Faction broodmares. Resistance was futile.

Natalia kicked the wall in frustration, the impact jarring her bones. She would never accept their right to take Earth's women and force them into a year of surrogacy. It was slavery masquerading as an honor.

Her thoughts turned to Rana. Had she escaped safely with her Tark mate? Natalia had risked everything to help her get away, even while doubting the young woman's assertion that she loved the alien who'd claimed her. She still believed Rana had been confused, brainwashed by whatever modification the Faction had done to make her able to carry hybrid young. No human in their right mind would ever willingly mate with one of those monsters.

A scraping sound at the entrance drew her from her thoughts. She turned to see the shimmering forcefield dissipate. Two Faction guards, a Brundle and an Alphan, entered, their impassive faces giving no hint of her fate.

"Prisoner Natalia Wilkes, you are summoned," said the Brundle, and his tone was as unreadable as his expression.

Natalia jutted out her chin defiantly as they clamped magnetic cuffs around her wrists. She would face her fate with pride, not cowering. She believed in her cause, even if it had doomed her. They led her from the cell down a maze of corridors. She studied her surroundings, watching for any opportunity to fight or flee, but found none. The Embassy was a fortress, inescapable for a lone human female.

After what seemed an interminable walk, they entered a large chamber outfitted with viewing screens along the walls. Natalia guessed it was some type of command center. Faction officers of various species stood around computing stations or studied data on the screens.

One screen showed a map of Earth with rotating statistics she couldn't decipher from this distance. Others displayed star charts and incomprehensible alien symbols. A third seemed to be the arrangement of Faction ships rotating around the planet. How she wished she could get this data to her rebel contacts.

At the far end of the room, upon a raised dais, stood a singular being. Natalia sucked in a shocked breath. It was a Serpentine, one of the cold-blooded reptilian Faction species she'd only heard vague rumors about. They rarely moved among Earthlings and seemed to keep to themselves.

The alien towered over the guards escorting her, well over seven feet tall. His skin was a deep emerald green with black striations and smooth and glossy like a serpent's. He appeared hairless. Nude from the waist up, his form displayed lean, rippling muscles she couldn't help noticing and admiring in spite of herself. A crest of small horns lined his head.

His eyes were the most striking. They were eclipse-black, with no visible pupils or irises. Still, she could feel the intensity of that fathomless gaze drilling into her.

Natalia suppressed a shudder at being so close to one of these fearsome aliens rarely seen by humans. She steeled herself, proudly lifting her chin as the guards brought her before him.

"General Zath, we have brought the prisoner as you commanded," said the Alphan.

The Serpentine dismissed them with a wave of his clawed hand, not taking his gaze from Natalia. She stood motionless, determined not to show fear.

Zath descended from the dais with predatory grace, slowly circling her in a sinuous, rippling movement. He had legs, but he moved so quickly that he might have been slithering like a common Earth snake. She could feel his gaze dragging over every inch of her body. Revulsion and anger swelled within her, along with something she didn't want to identify. How dare this creature ogle her so blatantly, as if she were no more than an animal to inspect?

"So, you are the one who presumed to steal Commander Sarko's mate." His voice was surprisingly mellow but with an underlying hiss, his sibilant voice echoing in the vast chamber.

Natalia said nothing, refusing to be baited. She stared straight ahead, her jaw clenched.

Zath halted directly in front of her, so close she could feel the chill emanating from his scaled skin. A long, thin tongue flicked out, nearly brushing her face. Testing her scent. "Such defiance," he murmured. "I admire it, even as I will crush it in time." A claw tipped her up chin.

She met the black mirrors of his eyes unflinchingly.

"For now, it pleases me to claim you as mine."

Natalia jerked back, shock and revulsion shooting through her. "Never," she spat. "I'll die first."

Zath's lipless mouth curved in a gruesome approximation of a smile. "You forget your place, little human. For your crime, your life belongs to the Faction now, to do with as we please. Be grateful you won't face execution for your treason."

Natalia trembled with impotent rage. To be given as spoils to this monster, forced to serve as his breeder slave...it was a fate worse than death.

Zath turned away, barking orders to his guards and officers. She sagged in her magnetic cuffs, despair threatening to overwhelm her defiance. This alien would use her body to plant his foul seed in her womb, and she was powerless to stop it.

The guards grasped her arms, marching her from the command center toward an unknown, horrific fate.

NATALIA SAT IN NUMB silence as the Mosaic Med Chief explained the genetic procedure she was about to undergo. Her mind rebelled at his clinical, dispassionate words.

"The process will rewrite your DNA just enough to make you compatible for breeding with General Zath. You will be able to safely carry Serpentine embryos to term and give birth. There should be no complications."

Just the obliteration of my humanity, she thought bitterly. Altered on a genetic level to become this monster's broodmare. She barely flinched as Quillen injected her with the modification serum. There was no escaping this violation of her body. She could only endure, hoarding her hatred, until the chance for vengeance presented itself.

The Mosiac studied his datascreen. "Excellent. The changes have begun. You'll stay here under observation for about an hour." His luminous golden eyes were sympathetic despite his clinical manner. "I know this is difficult but try to rest. The process can be taxing as your cells transform but is typically uncomplicated. My mate, Briana, handled it well, and I have never seen a serious reaction."

"Among all the women you've tortured and forced into breeding slavery? That's so reassuring."

He frowned slightly. "We mean you no harm, Natalia. Your match wants a family, and the Faction risked everything to save Earth."

"Certainly not from the kindness of your hearts." Without looking at him, she laid back on the exam table, turning away her face in dismissal. She would find no comfort or pity from those who served the Faction.

With a soft sigh, Quillen departed. The only sound remaining in the room was the soft hum of equipment monitoring her vitals.

Alone again, she slowed her breathing as exhaustion weighed upon her. It was a struggle to keep her eyes open. She suspected the "serum" also contained sedatives to keep her docile. Maybe they didn't do that to every proxy, but she was special, being part of the rebellion.

As darkness crept into the edges of her vision, she clung desperately to one thought before oblivion claimed her. Somehow, some way, she would make them pay.

NATALIA GRADUALLY BECAME aware of voices filtering through the fog veiling her mind. She kept her eyes closed, feigning continued unconsciousness as she strained to listen.

"The conversion was successful," said Quillen. "Her vitals are strong. She's ready for release, sir."

"Excellent," General Zath's hissing voice sent a spike of revulsion through Natalia. "I am eager to claim her, but I intend to be patient with this female. The goal is not just offspring but a willing mate."

Natalia nearly choked in dismay. This beast thought she would ever willing mate with him? She would rather die.

"A wise approach," said Quillen mildly. "It's unlikely but don't hesitate to bring her to our facility if complications arise."

"Thanks, Quillen. I'll take her from here."

Natalia struggled not to recoil as Zath's rough grasp closed around her arm. She blinked up at him, feigning dazed confusion.

"You belong to me now, little one," he said, studying her with those fathomless black eyes. "It's time you learned your true place."

She cast her gaze downward submissively, hiding her defiant thoughts. She would pretend to accept her fate but never give up seeking escape.

Natalia followed Zath silently as he led her through the polished corridors of the embassy. After several turns, they entered comfortable quarters outfitted with two bedrooms, a small table and chairs, a kitchenette, and a hygiene chamber.

"You will share my rooms during your time here," said Zath. "My sleeping chamber is beside yours should you require anything. There are garments and toiletries for you."

He gestured to the neatly folded stack of clothes and basic toiletries laid out. "I'll return shortly with a meal."

He departed without waiting for a response, the door sealing behind him. Natalia glanced around warily before sinking down on the edge of the bed. She had expected to be thrown into a cell or forced into his room and immediately mounted, not given private rooms. What game was Zath playing?

Suspicion warred with grudging relief at the chance to clean herself and change clothing after so long confined. Cautiously, she explored the hygiene chamber, finding the basics needed to wash and refresh herself. The promised garments were plain but comfortable and far better than her tattered rags.

When Zath returned, Natalia was seated rigidly at the table. He nodded in approval at her transformed appearance before placing a tray before her.

"Quillen recommended only light foods until your system stabilizes. I synthicated this soup and bread for you. Eat, and then rest."

Natalia eyed the steaming bowl distrustfully. Anything could be in it—more sedatives, or worse. Yet she was already so altered against her will that it hardly mattered now. Resigned, she lifted the spoon with a slightly unsteady hand to sip the fragrant broth.

She forced herself to eat slowly, though nausea roiled her empty stomach in protest. The meal was soon finished, her body craving more but she ignored that, not wanting to be ill since her stomach was still rocky.

Exhaustion pressed upon her, but she resisted the lure of the bed, sitting tensely in the chair. She would not sleep, vulnerable, while Zath was so close by. Natalia settled in to keep her silent watch.

She kept her stubborn vigil as the embassy night cycle commenced, though bone-deep weariness pressed upon her. She had no intention of sleeping in this monster's territory, no matter how exhausted she became. Hardship had taught her to seize what rest she could, but she couldn't afford to lower her guard.

SOME HOURS LATER, ZATH returned bearing another tray of soup and bread. Natalia jerked awake from a doze, mortified she had slipped into slumber against her will. "I'm not hungry."

The Serp sighed. "You require rest and nourishment to integrate the modifications." He shook his head. "Why do you resist?"

Natalia just shrugged, not meeting his gaze. In truth, she was wary of being drugged or violated in her sleep.

Zath studied her for a long moment before speaking again. "You have my oath no harm will come to you here. Please eat and sleep. Your health depends on it."

Though reluctant, Natalia's trembling hand lifted the spoon to sip the broth. Her abused stomach immediately knotted in protest, and she had to pause, breathing through waves of nausea.

His expression softened with concern. "Go slowly. Your system is still weak due to your stubbornness. No other human female has had side effects for so long after the injection, because they were sensible."

Natalia managed a few more spoonsful before pushing away the bowl, the measly portion already too much. Zath collected the dishes without comment and brought her a cup of medicinal tea instead.

"Drink this to settle your stomach. The nutrients will help you heal."

Too weary to resist, Natalia sipped the bittersweet liquid. Her eyelids soon grew heavy as it soothed her queasy stomach. She barely stirred when Zath carried her to the bed, covering her with a soft blanket.

"Rest well, brave Natalia," she heard him murmur before sleep claimed her.

OVER THE NEXT DAYS, Natalia continued resisting nourishment, suspicious of Zath's motives. He remained patient but firm, coaxing her to eat small amounts and drink the medicinal teas.

"You're only hurting yourself with this stubbornness," he said in quiet frustration after Natalia pushed away another barely touched meal.

"Maybe death would be preferable to being a slave," she said bitterly.

Zath regarded her somberly. "I vow you will be no slave of mine, Natalia. In time, you will come to see the truth and learn your place is beside me, not beneath me."

She blinked, staring at him for half a minute without speaking. How she longed for that to be true, so it would be easier to slip away from him. "I wish I could believe that, but I don't. You have too much to gain, and I have too much to lose if I capitulate."

He gave her a sad look and nodded once before leaving her room.

NATALIA WANTED TO CLING to her hatred, but Zath's gentle insistence on caring for her eroded her distrust bit by bit. One evening, he arrived bearing another bowl of light broth and hunks of soft bread. Natalia's stomach rumbled at the savory aroma, reminding her she'd managed only a few bites at the midday meal.

He seated himself across from her and broke off a piece of bread, holding it out with his clawed hand. "Just try a small amount. The synthicator is quite good at capturing the fresh-baked taste from my understanding. Serps don't eat bread though." He sounded almost regretful about that. "We are carnivores."

Too hungry to refuse, she took the offering and nibbled the edge. The fresh-baked taste exploded on her tongue. Before she knew it, she'd devoured the morsel. Zath gave an approving rumble, tearing off another chunk and passing it over. She hesitated only a moment before accepting it. Slowly, she finished the bread while he ate something that smelled like grilled meat.

When she'd cleaned her bowl of broth as well, he said, "Your appetite is improving. That's good."

She shrugged, unwilling to admit it was thanks to his insistent care. "I suppose living as your prisoner requires some effort to stay alive."

His expression became solemn. "I hope in time you won't see it that way. I aim to prove myself honorable, not the monster you believe me to be."

"Why does it matter what I think?" she asked with a trace of bitterness. "I'm just a slave to be used for a year."

He rose abruptly, his tail lashing in agitation. She tensed, instantly regretting her words, but he only paced to the window, gazing outside at the bustling human city below him without speaking for a long moment. "Such destruction."

"What?"

"Your cities and planet. They've endured much destruction, just like we all have, yet new life is returning. Amidst the rubble, PODs house humans and Faction alike. People strive to rebuild and cling to hope."

"I...yes, I guess so. What's your point?"

At last, he turned, his black serpentine eyes unreadable. His response didn't answer her question. "You are no slave. I hope someday, you will see me as more than the beast you expect. For now, I will wait."

With that, he excused himself, leaving Natalia to ponder his cryptic words. What did he hope she would see in him that she didn't already? And why did part of her wish to find out?

Chapter Two

JUST BEFORE MEETING Natalia...

Zath could scarcely contain his anticipation as he awaited Natalia's arrival. The chance to take a mate, something he'd never expected, filled him with fierce longing. The humans called it a "year of service" but to him, this female would be a lifemate if they were compatible.

He'd chosen carefully upon reviewing the candidates who would be easiest to modify for him. He'd been spoiled for choice, having four females from which to choose. He knew the proctors thought him crazy to have selected the defiant prisoner, but he'd sensed something special in her when he observed her fevered pacing from the security logs before making his decision. She had a warrior spirit and would birth strong hatchlings. His cold blood heated at the thought of claiming her soft body and planting his seed.

Yet he knew he must be patient. She was predisposed to hate him and wouldn't even want to mate with him for offspring, let alone to form a real relationship, at least, not yet. So, he would wait, wooing her until she came to accept him. Only then could they create a true bond.

At last, she arrived, led between guards, her blonde hair filthy and matted, body swallowed by tattered rags, but her chin was high, green eyes blazing, as she faced him without flinching.

Zath dismissed the guards, circling her slowly while admiring her courage. Her scent was strange yet alluring, a feminine musk mixing with her defiance. It stirred his primal serpent instincts to dominate, yet also triggered unfamiliar warmth.

She trembled with rage at his bold appraisal, though whether from fear or indignance, he did not know. Likely both. When she declared she'd rather die than be his, Zath was undeterred. Her fiery spirit only intrigued him more. She was untamed, a wild *vrash* forced into his nest. He would need to be cunning to make her accept him, but cleverness was the Serpentine's nature.

In time, she would come to crave his embrace and beg to bear his offspring. He was sure of it. The thought sent a heady rush of anticipation through his blood. For now, he would bide his time like the predator he was. His tenacity would win out eventually.

Zath approvingly noted her strength. Weaker spirits broke in this moment. When she dared speak bitterness against him, Zath only admired her defiance. She would never yield easily. His worthy mate.

NOW...

Zath studied Natalia closely as she picked at the meal he'd brought to her quarters. She ate little, but it was progress after many days of outright refusing sustenance.

Her blonde hair had regained some luster after he'd provided grooming amenities. The clean garments emphasized her delicate curves rather than obscuring them as her rags had. She was still far too thin and pale, with dark circles beneath those green eyes. Yet the defiant spark in their depths remained undimmed.

He kept his tone gentle, hiding his frustration. "You must eat to regain your strength. There is no shame in it."

Her glare could have melted his scales if he were a lesser being. "I won't subsist on the scraps of my captor to better serve his twisted purposes."

"You are no captive here," he said calmly. "In time, you will see the truth."

"The truth?" She shoved away the dish, appetite clearly lost. "The truth is, you've taken everything from me—my freedom, my body, and my future. Don't pretend your pretty cage changes that reality."

Zath rose swiftly, fighting to control the lash of anger in his tail. "I would treat you as a revered mate, not some lowly slave." He towered over her, though she didn't cower. "You try my limits, human."

Natalia stood abruptly, reckless challenge flashing in her eyes. "Then end this farce between us. Take what you will by force. It's what you conquerors do best, isn't it?"

They froze, gazes locked, as the air practically simmered between them. Then he turned away with a hiss of frustration. "I won't dishonor you, or myself. Even if you insist on provoking me to it."

He didn't miss the flicker of surprise that broke through her anger before her expression shuttered closed again. Without another word, he excused himself, shaken by how easily she could goad him. He would need to reinforce his patience and self-control. Much depended on it.

ZATH'S DETERMINATION to court Natalia was tested daily. She was as prickly as a *vrash* and twice as stubborn.

She was slow to trust, and he found it difficult to understand her perspective. Humans were so fragile to Serps. Yet they were resilient, adapting to the harsh conditions on their ravaged planet.

Humans were fascinating, with their varied skin tones and hair colors. Natalia's hair was golden like the sun, her eyes an unusual green. Her body was petite and delicate, yet she possessed a fierce spirit. So many emotions. It was perplexing to him, and he despaired of ever being able to understand her, or for her to understand him.

Still, he kept trying. A few afternoons later, she was reading in the main living area of his quarters when he arrived early, having finished his shift sooner than expected. She looked startled and a tad wary but didn't immediately flee to her room. He counted that as a victory.

"I bring gifts," he said, holding up a basket.

Natalia eyed it warily. "Gifts?"

"Human food items. I thought you might enjoy them." He looked down at the various items, finding most of them unappetizing to his carnivorous palate. "There are fruits, vegetables, and sweets. I was told these are favorites among humans."

Natalia approached slowly, peering into the basket. Her eyes widened as she recognized the contents. "How did you get all this? This stuff is hard to come by now."

He preened, pleased by her reaction. "I synthicated it, of course. We can make anything with the basic building blocks of life—or nutrients."

She looked surly for a moment. "The rebels don't usually have fully stocked synthicators, so I haven't had an apple in years." Her fingers hovered over it as though she was at war with herself.

"It's yours," he said gently. "Please, eat."

Natalia snatched the fruit, biting into it with relish. Juice ran down her chin, and she licked it away, moaning softly. The sound made both of his hemipenes spasm and start to stiffen, and he struggled to hide the reaction.

"This is delicious," she said, taking another bite. "Thank you."

Zath inclined his head. "I am glad you're enjoying it. There is more where it came from." He froze in surprise when she cautiously extended the apple in his direction.

"Would you like a bite?" She seemed almost shy about asking.

Though he didn't require fruit, he leaned forward, taking a cautious bite. The crisp flesh burst with sweet juice on his tongue, and he made a sound of pleasure. "I see why you enjoy this. The texture is interesting, though it does nothing for my nutritional requirements."

She laughed. "If you want empty calories..." Her fingers hovered over the basket for a moment until she selected a chocolate. Seemingly on impulse, she brought it to his lipless mouth herself. "Try this."

He opened to allow her to place the morsel inside. The rich flavor exploded on his forked tongue, and he moaned in appreciation. "That is truly exquisite. Sweet and decadent."

Her eyes gleamed with amusement. "I think you like human food as much as we do."

"Perhaps I do." He lowered his voice, leaning in closer. "But there is one thing I like even more."

Natalia's pulse visibly pounded, and her pheromones changed, perfuming the air and making him flick out his tongue to taste/scent her. His hemipenes swelled, aching to emerge.

To his disappointment, Natalia stepped back, breaking the spell. "I should...go rest."

"Of course," he said, keeping his voice calm. "I will see you at the evening meal."

"Yes." She fled to her room, leaving Zath to wonder if he'd pushed too hard. Perhaps she needed more time to adjust to her new life, but he feared losing her to the past.

OVER THE NEXT WEEKS, he continued to pursue Natalia. He brought her treats, offered to spend time with her, and tried to engage her in conversation. She was still reserved, but he finally managed to draw her into a real conversation as he discussed the Serp homeworld, long destroyed by the Vorathans. "It was a red desert planet with an ultraviolet sun that glowed purple. Our people lived underground in vast caverns where our ancestors built magnificent cities."

Natalia listened, clearly fascinated. "Did you have families like we do?"

"Our social structure was similar, yes. Clutchmates were born in the same clutch, and we formed lifelong bonds with our siblings. The males were trained to fight, and the females were raised to be nurturers and caretakers."

"So, women were second-class citizens?" she asked with clear disapproval.

"No, not at all." He shook his head. "We valued all roles equally. The females ruled the clutches, and the matriarchs held great power. My mother, Zaria, was a formidable female, and she wouldn't hesitate to confront any male who displeased her."

Natalia relaxed. "That sounds a lot like human society. Women are often underestimated, but they can be deadly when crossed."

Was there a note of warning in her tone? He struggled not to smile. "Indeed. I have no doubt you're capable of such."

"Damn right," she muttered. "I'm no one's victim."

"I would never presume otherwise. You are a fierce warrior, and I admire you for it." He kept his tone sincere and respectful. His admiration was genuine.

Natalia flushed, looking down at her hands. "You're not what I expected."

"I hope that's a good thing." He cocked his head. "You are also unlike what I expected. I find you intriguing."

"Me? Why?"

"You're intelligent and passionate. Not to mention beautiful. Any male would be fortunate to claim you." He cleared his throat. "Unlike many of my brethren, I had a choice of mates to select, and I chose you. The proctors must have thought me mad since you were in a cell and are deeply involved with the rebellion against our presence."

Her eyes narrowed. "Not against your presence. Just the truce our government signed on our behalf without giving women any choice." She sighed. "I don't understand you. I don't understand this." She gestured to the luxury around them. "I don't understand any of this."

"What do you not understand?"

Natalia shrugged, avoiding his gaze. "Why do bloodthirsty warriors want families? Is it just to perpetuate another generation of bloodshed?"

His eyes narrowed, and his tail lashed in his agitation. "We are hardly bloodthirsty. The Vorathans invaded our worlds before Earth, and we fought back once we banded together. We have lost much to the war with them, and to ensure they remain banished to the outer edges of the galaxy. I can't speak for all the Faction's warriors, but for myself, I simply want a peaceful existence developing my designated land on Baxa when my final Earth rotation ends in two years. I want a family at my side as I do that."

"Oh." She looked down at her hands. "I'm sorry that I didn't realize. I assumed you were all conquering monsters."

"Our people were never predominantly warriors, but the Vorathans left us little choice. They are a brutal species that cares only for conquest and domination. They destroy entire planets and enslave their inhabitants. We have only ever sought to protect ourselves and others from their depravity."

Natalia's shoulders slumped. "I had no idea. The rebels have always portrayed the Faction as selfish invaders, only slightly better than the Vorathans. I guess I should have known better."

"You were misled, as are many humans." He reached out, cupping her cheek. "You aren't to blame for your ignorance, and I don't believe any of the rebels are deliberately providing bad information. It must be terrible from human females' viewpoints to have to give your body and a year of your life to provide offspring for aliens." He paused. "I would like to show you something, if you will permit it."

Natalia nodded, curious. He took her hand, leading her to the balcony. She tensed, clearly expecting to be taken outside, but he only drew her into the shadows of the doorway.

"Look." He pointed at a distant hillside, where a group of Faction and human children played together. Their laughter drifted on the breeze, and Natalia smiled.

"Those younglings are the future serf both our races. The Faction and human governments agreed to this treaty for the mutual benefit of both sides. In time, this world will become a thriving metropolis, and you will be a part of it." He struggled to control his emotions for a moment. "*We* will be part of it if your womb is blessed. I have taken you as a proxy, but I hope to make you a mate."

Natalia's eyes widened in shock as she reared back from him. "A mate?"

"Yes. If you will have me." He bowed his head. "I desire a partner, not just a surrogate, and that is my ultimate goal. I believe we can be happy together if you can give us a chance. If not, I will have to accept your departure at the end of our year together, unless you are pregnant. Then we'll part after the baby's birth." He grimaced, already hating the idea. She smelled so delicious, so right to him, that he couldn't believe she wasn't meant to be at his side for a lifetime.

"I...don't know what to say," she whispered. "I never expected this."

"Neither did I, but I cannot deny my feelings." He pulled her close, inhaling her scent. "I think you feel the connection too, or you would have rejected me outright."

She blushed, pulling away. "I don't know what I feel. Everything is so confusing. Can you give me time to sort it out?"

He nodded. "Of course. I won't pressure you, but I hope you'll consider my offer. I promise you won't regret it."

She gave him a tentative smile. "Thank you."

He nearly groaned when her pink tongue flicked out to lick her plump lips. Imagining it swirling around one of his hemipenes while her hand massaged the other made him suddenly desperate for relief. "If you will excuse me..." Beating a hasty retreat, he rushed to his bedroom, closing the door behind him.

He stripped off his clothing, freeing his swollen hemipenes that had burst through the slits from the pouch where they normally nestled. One was already leaking precum, and he stroked it roughly, imagining it was Natalia's soft hand instead. He hissed, stroking faster, and his other hemipene emerged, dripping copiously.

He gripped them both, rubbing them together, and imagined Natalia kneeling before him, her lush lips wrapped around his shafts. No, she'd only be able to take one at most, but her tongue could explore both. Her green eyes would gaze up at him, her cheeks hollowed as she sucked him.

Zath let out a strangled moan, coming hard with one hemipene and spurting his seed all over his hand. He shuddered, continuing to stroke even when the bedroom door opened behind him. He turned halfway toward her, his hemipenes in his hands, still pulsing and twitching as he climaxed from his second hemipene.

Natalia's eyes widened, her face flushing with color. She stared for a long moment before turning and fleeing.

He cursed, quickly cleaning himself off and dressing. When he went after her, she was in her own room, the door closed. He knocked, and she answered, her expression unreadable.

"I'm sorry you saw that," he said awkwardly. "I was overcome by the need—"

She interrupted, clearly trying to sound blasé, though she was flushing. "I've seen men masturbate before, at least from a distance."

"You have?" He frowned. "Who?" He sounded angry, but he was simply alarmed by the idea of men so blatantly doing such a thing in a female's presence.

"Men in the rebel camps. It's not uncommon, especially in winter, when we're cold and miserable." She shrugged. "It's hard to be discreet when there are many people surrounding you."

"I see." His unease settled, and he felt foolish. "I apologize for my reaction."

She swallowed, looking fearful. "Look, you might as well know it now…" She swallowed, clearly gathering her courage as he held his breath, wondering if she was about to refuse all consideration of being more than his surrogate, or anything else. If she chose not to let him have access to her body, he'd already decided he wouldn't enforce his right to do so. The truce didn't give him justification to force her in his mind, and they would be roommates for the remainder of her proxy year.

The thought pained him, and he held his breath.

Chapter Three

WHY HAD SHE FOLLOWED him and then entered without knocking? He'd left so abruptly that she'd been concerned something was wrong with Zath, and it had felt natural to check on him. When had she started to care about his wellbeing?

Two cocks. Good lord, how was she supposed to handle that? She nearly fainted at the thought, comparing it to the one lackluster cock she's taken a few times before. Rich couldn't compare to one of his, let alone both.

Which brought her back to her confession. "I never planned to be caught or used as a surrogate, so I didn't follow the most basic law." She notched up her chin as she met his black eyes. "I'm not a virgin."

Zath didn't seem surprised. "I suspected as much. It matters little. The modifications will ensure you are fertile."

She frowned in confusion, deciding he had to know everything. "That's not what I mean. I'm saying I'm not a virgin because I've had sex before."

"I assumed that's what you meant by not being a virgin." He sounded almost amused.

She scowled. "It's a big deal to you guys. The Faction treaty stipulates I'm supposed to remain a virgin until my term of service window ends at twenty-five."

He shrugged. "How old are you?"

"Twenty-six, but I had sex when I was twenty-one." She was defiant about it but also a little embarrassed now that she was telling him. Rich had been a fellow rebel, and she suspected she'd responded to his overtures more as a way to give the Faction the middle finger than because she'd truly wanted her fellow activist.

His mouth twitched. "If you had sex five years ago, I have no fear that you might be pregnant with a human child now, do I?"

"Uh, no." She blinked, realizing he truly didn't care. "You really don't. Why?"

He shrugged. "I understand the reason for maintaining virginity in the human surrogates, but that experience is in your distant past. You aren't pregnant with another's child, so your womb is available to my seed. That's what our agreement is—though I want much more than a proxy, as I said."

Natalia was unsettled by his relaxed attitude. "I expected you to report me to the Faction Embassy or Earth government."

"For what? Having consensual sex with a human male? I fail to see why that would be of interest to anyone."

She gaped at him. "Are you serious? The treaty says—"

"It says human females must be virgins between the ages of eighteen and twenty-five." He cocked his head. "I don't care if you've had sex with every male on this planet before me. All I care about is that you are here with me now, and that you'll bear my offspring."

"I'm not sure if I should be relieved or insulted." She folded her arms across her chest. "You act like it doesn't matter that I've had sex before, but I'm pretty sure it does. Your Faction—"

Zath sighed, looking vaguely irritated. "Does not speak for me personally in all matters, *vrash*."

"What does *vrash* mean?" She frowned.

"It means female, but with a connotation of being a stubborn creature with a sharp tongue." He looked amused. "I would not have chosen you if you were weak-willed or easily cowed. I admire your spirit, and I am proud to call you mine."

Natalia was taken aback. "I'm not yours."

"Yet," he said with certainty. "Soon, you will be, but in the meantime, I am content to court you. I wish to win your heart, not your body alone."

"You're not going to try to force yourself on me?" She was still suspicious despite his words.

"No." He looked disgusted. "I would never dishonor either of us that way. I seek a true mate, not a *vrushta* to rut with and discard."

She winced at the word, knowing it was an insult in the context, though she'd never heard it before. "I'm not a whore."

"I know. You are a strong female, and I respect you. You're loyal to your cause, and I understand that. Sex is a normal function, and I don't consider you a whore or any other shaming word for indulging. I would have you willing and eager, or not at all."

"Oh." She was at a loss for words. "I don't know what to say." He was so different from what she'd expected.

"Say you will allow me to court you, and that you will consider becoming my mate when our year is complete." His expression was earnest.

"I...yes, I will." She didn't know what else to say. It seemed the least she could do to repay his kindness, since he clearly wasn't the cold beast she'd assumed him to be. He was multifaceted and alluring in his own way.

He smiled, revealing his fangs. "I am pleased. Thank you, Natalia."

"You're welcome." She hesitated. "I shouldn't ask, but..." She licked her lips, her core pulsing as she recalled what she'd seen moments before. "Do you really have two cocks?"

Zath's eyes gleamed. "Yes. Would you like to see them?"

She flushed. "Maybe."

"Then come with me." He led her to her bed and sat, beckoning her to join him. Natalia perched on the edge of the mattress, watching as he unfastened his pants, revealing the twin cocks she'd glimpsed earlier.

Her eyes widened. "They're huge."

"They are of average size for a Serp." He stroked them slowly, one in each hand, and Natalia watched, mesmerized, as they became long and hard. Her pussy clenched, and she squirmed, feeling a rush of wetness between her thighs. "We call them hemipenes. One emerges from each slit in the pouch of our groin. I can use them separately or together."

"Together?" She gulped, imagining the stretch. "How?"

Zath shifted, lying back and spreading his legs. "Like this." He guided one of his hemipenes to the other, rubbing them together. The tips kissed, and a clear fluid leaked from both. "This is lubricant. It eases penetration."

"I see." Her voice was a mere whisper, and she couldn't look away.

"Would you like to touch them?" His voice was deep and seductive.

"Yes." She reached out, running a fingertip along the tip of one. Zath moaned, and she jerked back her hand. "Did I hurt you?"

"No. The opposite. It feels good when you touch them."

"Oh." She touched the other, circling the broad tip. Zath's breathing grew ragged, and she liked the power she wielded. "What happens next?"

"I penetrate you with one and stimulate the other with my hand, or..." He paused. "I could suckle it."

"Suckle it?" Her eyes widened. "With your mouth?"

"Yes. Serps can form a seal with their mouths, and we have a flexible, muscular tongue that can wrap around a shaft." He blinked as his tongue flicked out. "If my partner is willing, I can also penetrate with both hemipenes simultaneously."

"Both?" She gulped, unable to imagine the sensation. "At the same time? How?"

Zath smirked. "I could show you."

Natalia's entire body heated as she imagined his tongue and cocks inside her. "I..." She licked her lips. "Okay." Why not? She was here to do just this for a year. Maybe it wouldn't be as terrible or frightening as she'd anticipated.

Zath's eyes gleamed, and his hemipenes further stiffened. "Take off your clothes and lie on the bed."

She obeyed, removing her shirt and trousers. Her nipples hardened in the cool air, and she shivered.

"Lie down." He waited until she was in position before joining her. "Open your legs for me."

Natalia spread her knees, exposing her pussy. She was already damp, and her clit throbbed with need. She resisted the urge to shield herself when she saw his hunger. She was doing this because she was curious, and because she wanted to touch him, so hiding her nudity would be counterproductive.

Zath moved between her thighs, his dark gaze locked on hers. "I will pleasure you first, and then I will claim you."

She nodded but cleared her throat. "Humans like a little touching and kissing before going below the waist."

"Ah, I see." He leaned down, brushing his mouth against hers. Natalia's eyes widened when his tongue flicked out, licking her lips. He tasted surprisingly sweet, and she opened to him, allowing him to explore her mouth. His tongue was long and agile, and it caressed her own, making her moan.

His lipless mouth pressed against hers, the kiss surprisingly sensual despite the differences in their anatomy. She reached up, tracing the line of his jaw and the smooth scales of his neck. He purred, the sound vibrating through her, and she gasped.

Zath broke the kiss, looking down at her with glowing eyes. A luminescent green had appeared in the previously all-black orbs. "You taste delicious, *vrash*."

Natalia's face warmed. "So do you."

"I want to taste more of you." Zath trailed kisses down her neck, pausing to nuzzle the sensitive spot where it joined her shoulder. "Here." He licked the spot, making her shiver. "And here." He continued down her body, stopping to tease each nipple. "And here." He licked her belly, and she giggled, ticklish. "And here." He settled between her thighs, gazing at her pussy. "But most of all, I want to taste you here."

Natalia's eyes widened when his tongue snaked out, flicking her clit. "Oh, my..." She arched, gasping at the sensation. "That feels so good."

Zath made a sound of pleasure, his tongue delving deeper. He lapped at her folds, exploring every inch of her intimate flesh with his agile appendage. Natalia writhed, moaning, as he found her entrance and thrust inside.

"Zath." She clutched at his head, lightly cupping his hairless skull. "Please, more."

He obliged, fucking her with his tongue. The flexible muscle curled inside her, finding her G-spot and pressing against it. She cried out, her hips bucking as she came. Zath continued to lap at her, drawing out her orgasm until she was limp and sated.

He lifted his head, his eyes gleaming with satisfaction. "You taste divine, *vrash*."

Natalia blushed, her body humming with pleasure. "You're good at that."

"I enjoy pleasuring you." He crawled up her body, bracing himself above her. "Now, I will claim you."

"Yes." Natalia gazed up at him, her heart pounding. "Make me yours."

Zath's eyes flashed, and he growled, his hemipenes fully emerging from their slits. They were thick and ridged, and Natalia's eyes widened at the sight.

"Will they fit?" She was suddenly nervous.

"Yes, *vrash*. I will take my time and prepare you." He reached between her thighs, stroking her slick folds. "I promise not to harm you."

Natalia relaxed, trusting him. "Okay."

Zath continued to stroke her, his fingers teasing her clit and dipping into her channel. Natalia moaned, arching into his touch. "More."

He obliged, adding a third finger to the mix. "This first time, I'll only claim you with one pene."

"One pene?" She panted, her body on fire. "Will that satisfy you?"

"For now." He withdrew his fingers, positioning the tip of one pene at her entrance. "Relax, *vrash*. I won't hurt you."

"I trust you." Natalia exhaled, forcing herself to relax. She was nervous but excited.

Zath pushed inside her, and she gasped at the stretch. He was much larger than the one human male she'd been with, and the sensation of fullness was overwhelming. "That's just one?" She was close to sobbing for a moment, feeling defeated.

"Yes, and I haven't even gotten it in all the way yet." He chuckled. "I'll go slowly."

"I can handle it." She was determined to prove it.

"I know you can, but I want you to enjoy this." He began to move, and she groaned, her body adjusting to his size.

"That's it, *vrash*. Take me in." He rocked his hips, pushing deeper. Natalia moaned, her body stretching to accommodate him.

"You feel so good." Zath's eyes were half-closed, his expression one of bliss. "So tight and hot."

She clung to him, her nails digging into his scaled shoulders. "More."

He growled, increasing his pace. "You're so beautiful. I can't get enough of you."

Natalia moaned, arching beneath him. "Yes. I want you." It was humbling but somehow freeing to admit that to him.

His eyes glowed, and he leaned down to capture her mouth in a searing kiss. His tongue plunged into her mouth, mimicking the movement of his cock in her pussy.

Which made her think of his other pene, currently neglected. Fumbling somewhat clumsily, she grasped the smooth, thick shaft, making him hiss in pleasure.

"*Vrash*." He shuddered, his eyes closing as she stroked him. "You undo me."

"I want to please you." She tightened her grip, pumping him faster.

"You do." He groaned, his hips jerking. "I'm close."

"Come for me, Zath." She urged him on, and he grunted, his cock pulsing in her hand. He spurted, coating her hand and belly with his seed. Natalia gasped, the warm liquid sending a thrill through her.

The cock inside her was still hard and throbbing. He thrust into her again. "Keep going. I'm not done."

"Yes." She met his thrusts, her body singing with pleasure. "Harder."

He complied, driving into her with abandon. Her inner walls clenched around him, and she came with a cry, her body shuddering in ecstasy. He followed soon after, his release triggering another wave of pleasure for her.

Natalia collapsed, spent. "Holy..."

"I agree." Zath rolled off her, panting. "That was intense."

"Yeah." She stared at the ceiling, her mind reeling. "I didn't expect that."

"Neither did I." He turned to her, his expression serious. "Are you all right?"

"I'm fine." She smiled, reaching for his hand without thinking. "I just...that was extraordinary."

"It was." He squeezed her hand, his eyes glowing. "I hope we can do it again in a little bit."

"Me too." She blushed, realizing she meant it. "Do you have um, quick, recovery time?"

He chuckled. "I do tonight." He put her hand over his pouch, where his hemipenes were retreating, and they started to get hard again.

Her eyes widened, but she didn't shy away. "We can do that again then."

"Soon." He stood, offering her a hand. "You must be starving. I know I am. Let me synthicate us some food, and then we can talk...and later..."

Natalia nodded, her stomach growling in agreement even as her sated core pulsed with renewed interest. "Thank you." While he left her bedroom to go to the kitchenette, she went to the bathroom to clean up, taking a moment to study her reflection in the mirror. She looked the same, but she felt different. She was no longer a rebel. Now, she was a proxy—and, if she was honest, she didn't feel like a prisoner.

She felt cherished and protected. Safe.

Loved?

The thought was worrisome, and she didn't dwell on it as she finished cleaning herself and dressing before going to join him.

Zath was waiting for her in the kitchenette, a plate of steaming food on the table. "Sit, *vrash*. Eat."

She sat, inhaling the fragrant aroma of the food. "It smells delicious."

"It is a traditional Serp dish. *Kavla,* spicy style." He sat across from her, watching as she took a bite.

It was spicy but flavorful, and her eyes widened. "It's good."

"I'm glad you like it, since it is one of my favorites." He smiled, his fangs flashing. "Perhaps you might not want to know the source."

Her stomach clenched as she put down her fork. "What is it?"

"A desert rodent from my homeworld, but this is just a synthicated version of its molecular composition, of course. Like most life on my world, *kavla* have gone extinct."

Sadness filled her at the words. "Earth has lost many species since the Vorathan invasion, though I don't think we were particularly careful with the life around us before invasion. My grandmother told me stories of before, but I can barely remember a time when we weren't at war." She blinked back sudden tears.

His expression softened. "You lived with your grandmother?"

She nodded. "My parents were involved in fighting the Vorathans. My father died months before the Faction came, and then my mother..."

He looked sympathetic. "She died?"

She shook her head and took a deep breath, bracing herself to make the admission. "She was and is a leader of the resistance against the Faction. When I was twelve, she sent me to live with my grandmother, who died when I was seventeen. Mom had me return then, and I naturally became part of the resistance." How would he react to that?

"I see." His expression was neutral. "And now you are here."

She nodded, her chest tight. "I've been a rebel all my life. It's all I know."

"I understand. I was a juvenile when the Vorathans invaded my world. The Faction found me, but the only path forward was as a warrior. I fought alongside the others, and I earned a place in the Faction. It was my life until I was given this opportunity."

"To have a surrogate?" She frowned. "I don't understand why you'd choose that over mating with a Serp female."

"There are few of us left, and fewer females. We are a dying race, and we need to find a way to survive." He looked solemn. "The solution was Earth, but we didn't undertake the truce lightly, Natalia. We understand what we're asking from human women, but our survival depends on it. So did Earth's until we interceded with the Vorathans. You might not believe it, but you owe us your very existence."

"I know that," she said quietly. "I'm not ungrateful, but I'm not happy about being forced to breed either."

"I understand, and I'm sorry. It's not an ideal situation, but it's the best option for both our races. In time, I hope you can be happy with me. I care for you, Natalia."

She swallowed, her emotions in turmoil. "I care for you too, Zath."

He smiled, his eyes lighting up. "I'm glad. Perhaps someday, you will love me."

"Perhaps." She wasn't ready to admit it, but she was falling for the handsome Serp. How that could be possible, she didn't know, but she couldn't deny her feelings.

"In the meantime, let's enjoy the time we have together. I have a few tasks I must see to after dinner, but I'd like you to consider sharing my room and my bed."

She blinked. "Your room?"

"Yes. It's more comfortable than the guest quarters, and I'd like you to be near me." His expression was earnest. "I understand if you're not ready, but I'd like you to think about it."

She swallowed, her heart pounding. "What will you do if I refuse?"

"Nothing. You are free to make your own decisions, *vrash*. You aren't a slave, nor a prisoner. You're my proxy, and I will treat you as such. I hope by now you understand your place—beside me."

She blinked, surprised. "Really?"

"Of course. I would never force myself on you, and I would never force you to do anything you didn't want to do. If you wish to remain in the guest quarters, that is your choice." He wiped his mouth as he finished eating. "I will respect your wishes, but I would prefer you share my room and my bed."

Natalia nodded. "I'll think about it."

"That's all I ask." He stood, carrying their dishes to the sink. "I'll be back in a couple of hours."

"Okay." She watched as he left, conflicted. Part of her wanted to run, but another part wanted to stay. She was confused, and she didn't know what to do. What she wanted conflicted with everything she'd believed, so how did she reconcile that?

Chapter Four

ZATH DIDN'T REALLY have duties. He just wanted to give her time to process the abrupt changes between them. He needed perspective too.

That was how he found himself in the Embassy recreation hub, sharing a drink with Grand Admiral Pate.

"I'm concerned," said the older Grimlock. "I've heard you chose a rebel as your proxy. I worry for your safety, Zath."

"I appreciate your concern, but I'm well aware of the risks." Zath sipped his drink, a potent concoction of fermented fruits native to the planet. "I'm not afraid of the rebels."

"You should be." Pate's eyes narrowed. "They're unpredictable and desperate. They've already proven they're willing to kidnap proxies."

He nodded, smiling. "I spoke with Commander Sarko's mate before selecting Natalia. She told me the rebels thought they were rescuing her, and Natalia helped her return to Sarko when she learned Rana didn't want to be 'rescued.'"

Pate raised an eyebrow. "Interesting. The human female was able to sway the rebels?"

"Yes, or at least Natalia. The resistance has good reason to resent their government agreeing to this arrangement on their behalf, but I think the way to peace is to prove ourselves and our intentions one proxy at a time."

"I agree. It's slow, but it's working." He paused. "What do you intend to do with Natalia?"

"I plan to keep her as my proxy, but I won't force her to do anything she doesn't want to do. I'm trying to win her heart."

Pate looked amused. "I wish you luck. From what I've seen, human females are strong-willed and independent."

"So are Serp females, but I've never known one who wouldn't want to be courted." He shrugged. "I have a year to convince her, and I intend to use every day of it."

"Just be careful. The rebellion isn't going away, and neither are the extremists. There are those among the Faction who would see them destroyed if it led to our destruction too."

"Sir, I don't know if that's true. Natalia's mother is a leader of the rebellion, and I don't think she wants to destroy us. She wants to save her people, as we do. I believe the key to peace lies in showing them we aren't their enemy."

Pate looked thoughtful. "You might be right, but it's a risk. Are you willing to take it?"

Zath nodded. "I am. Natalia is worth the risk."

"Then I wish you success." Pate raised his glass in a toast. "To your future together."

Zath clinked his glass against the other male and drank. "Thank you."

They talked for a while longer, and then Zath excused himself. He was eager to return to Natalia.

When he arrived at his quarters, he paused in the doorway of his bedroom, surprised to see Natalia sleeping in his bed. She looked peaceful with her blonde hair spread out on the pillow. Her lips were slightly parted, and she was breathing deeply.

He smiled, feeling a surge of affection for her. She was beautiful and strong, and he admired her courage. He was determined to win her heart, and he was confident he could do it. He undressed and climbed into bed beside her, careful not to wake her. He lay there, watching her sleep, and eventually drifted off himself, cocooned in the contentment of the moment.

THE NEXT MORNING, NATALIA woke him with a kiss. "Good morning."

His eyes flew open, and he smiled up at her. "Good morning, *vrash*. Did you sleep well?"

"I did." She grinned. "Your bed is much more comfortable than the one in the guest room."

"I'm glad you approve." He pulled her closer, kissing her. "I enjoy having you in my bed."

"I like it too." She nuzzled his neck, inhaling his scent, which made his hemipenes emerge from their slits.

"Mmm, *vrash*." He ran a hand down her back, cupping her ass. "I want you."

"I want you too." She straddled him, rubbing her pussy against his cocks. It was a long time before they left the bed.

Chapter Five

NATALIA TRIED TO CLING to her preconceptions over the next few weeks, but it proved impossible as she got to know him better. He was kind, patient, and surprisingly funny. He treated her like a queen, showering her with gifts and attention. He was also an attentive lover, always putting her pleasure first. She found herself falling for him despite her reservations.

One night, as they lay together in bed, he asked her a question that caught her off guard. "Do you miss your friends?"

She blinked, surprised. "My friends?"

"From the rebellion. The ones you were with when we captured you."

"Oh. Yes, I do." She swallowed, her throat suddenly tight. "Why do you ask?"

"I was wondering if you would like to see them."

"I would, yes." She was shocked. "You'd allow me to see them?"

"Of course. You're not a prisoner. You're my proxy, and I want you to be happy." His tongue trailed across her shoulder. "I hope you might visit them and see if your mother will consent to a summit with us."

"A summit?" She was incredulous. "You want to meet with my mom?"

"Yes. I think it's time to end the conflict between our peoples. Your mother is a powerful leader, and I believe she could help us reach a lasting peace."

Natalia hesitated, unsure. "I'm not sure she'd agree to it."

"Will you ask her?" He kissed her neck, making her shiver. "Please, *vrash*?"

"I'll try." She sighed, giving in. "I can't promise anything."

"That's all I ask." He smiled, his eyes glowing.

She smiled, her heart swelling with emotion. "You're serious, right? This isn't a way to track me as I lead you to them and scoop up everyone?"

He scowled. "No. I want peace, as do you. I think your mother is the key to that. Will you speak with her and tell her I want to meet?"

"I will, but I can't guarantee she'll agree." Rosalie was even more stubborn than her.

"I know, but it's a start." He brushed his mouth against her lips. "Thank you, Natalia."

"You're welcome." She was still reeling from the revelation. "I can't believe you're serious."

"I am."

"I have to go alone with no tracking tech." She slanted a glance at him. "You have to trust me to return. I could disappear and never come back."

"I trust you, Natalia." His eyes glowed with that green inner light. "I know you'll return to me."

Natalia's heart skipped a beat. "How can you be so certain?"

"Because you're mine, and I'm yours." He kissed her, his tongue tangling with hers. "You belong with me, *vrash*, and I'll wait for you."

Natalia's eyes stung with unshed tears. "I don't deserve your faith in me."

"You deserve the universe, Natalia." His eyes glowed with an inner light. "I will fight for you, even if you leave me. I love you."

The words made her tremble. "I love you too." She buried her face in his chest, her heart aching. "I never wanted to love you, but I do. I just need to convince my mother of that," she said with a weak smile as she lifted her head to look down at him.

"I understand." He stroked her hair, his touch soothing. "I'll wait for you, *vrash*. Always."

Natalia closed her eyes, savoring the moment. Despite the circumstances, she was happy. She had found a home with Zath, and she was content. Could it be possible to find peace that would extend the contentment, or would she have to give up something to be with him? The thought pained her, but she already knew what she'd choose if it came to that point. The man beside her offered everything she didn't know she'd wanted and now couldn't live without.

A COUPLE OF HOURS LATER, she left the Embassy and blended in with the foot traffic as she made her way to the tunnels under the city. She knew the route by heart, having used it countless times to move around the city unseen.

As she walked, she wondered if her mother would agree to a meeting with Zath. It was a risky proposition, but it could lead to peace. The thought of reconciliation between the humans and the Faction was appealing, but her mother would be skeptical.

Natalia reached the entrance to the tunnel and slipped inside, the darkness enveloping her. She moved quickly, knowing the guards patrolled the area regularly. She kept to the shadows, avoiding detection.

After a few minutes, she emerged from the tunnel and made her way to the central meeting point. It was an abandoned warehouse in the industrial district, and it was crawling with rebels. When she entered, she immediately caught sight of her mother at the back of the large room, conferring with a small group. "Mom." She lifted a hand and waved in her direction.

"Natalia?" Rosalie rushed forward, embracing her. "I thought you were dead, darling."

Natalia hugged her mother. "I'm fine."

"The Faction arrested you. I've been waiting for them to announce your sentence so we could save you." Rosalie's eyes narrowed. "What happened?"

"I was claimed as a proxy by a Serp general. Zath." Natalia swallowed.

Her mother's eyes widened. "You're mated to a Serp?"

"Not exactly. Right now, I'm officially just his proxy to produce offspring. After a year, I can choose to stay with him permanently."

Rosalie frowned. "I see. And you're considering it?"

"Yes." Natalia met her gaze. "I love him, Mom."

"Love?" Rosalie shook her head. "You can't love a monster."

"Zath isn't a monster. He's kind and gentle, and he treats me like a queen. He's nothing like the stories we've been told." She took a deep breath. "He wants to meet with you. He wants peace."

"Peace?" Rosalie snorted. "They want to conquer us, Natalia. Don't be fooled."

"I'm not. I know they want to breed with us, but they're not the monsters you think they are. If they wanted to conquer us, they wouldn't have negotiated a treaty or saved Earth from the Vorathans. They could have let us die, but they didn't. They intervened, and now they're offering us a chance at a better life. We can't keep fighting forever, Mom. We have to find a way to coexist, and this is the first step."

Rosalie's expression was unreadable. "You really believe that, don't you?"

"I do." Natalia met her gaze. "I know you're skeptical, but I'm asking you to consider it. Please, Mom. Give him a chance, for me."

Rosalie sighed. "I can't make any promises, but I'll think about it."

"That's all I ask." Natalia embraced her mother. "I love you, Mom."

"I love you too, baby."

The word made her stiffen as she contemplated telling her mother she suspected she was pregnant. No, she should tell Zath first and had only held off because she'd worried he wouldn't let her come alone to her mom if she told him she suspected she was expecting before she came to see her mother.

She'd been nauseated for days and had missed her last period, which was unusual for her. She hadn't mentioned it to Zath, but she suspected he knew something was different. He was perceptive like that. "You'll meet with him, won't you, Mom?" she asked, trying to convince her mother. She had deeply personal reasons to want the truce with expecting a baby. She wanted her mate and her mother to be part of its life.

"I'll think about it. I'm not sure I can trust him. Any of them." Rosalie's expression was guarded. "You know how I feel about the Faction."

"I know, but this could be a chance for peace. I want both of you in my life. I don't want to choose."

Rosalie bit her lip and sighed. "I understand, but I need to be cautious. I can't risk the safety of our people."

She nodded. "I know, but please do it. For me. I'm asking you to trust me."

Rosalie sighed. "Fine. I'll meet with him, but I make no guarantees."

"That's all I ask." She smiled in relief and hugged the older woman again. "Thank you, Mom."

"Don't thank me yet. We still have a lot of work to do." Her expression was grim. "The rebels aren't going to give up easily, and neither are the Faction."

"I know, but we have to try. It's the only way forward." Natalia's voice was firm.

"I hope you're right, darling." Her voice softened. "I want you to be happy, and I'm glad you found someone who treats you well. I just have to get used to the idea of my little girl being mated to a Serp."

"I know it's a lot to take in, but I think this could be the beginning of a new era for both our peoples. We have a chance to build a better future for everyone, and I want to be part of that." Natalia smiled, her eyes shining. "I love you, Mom, and I want peace for everyone."

"I love you too, baby." Rosalie's eyes misted as she embraced her daughter. "I'm proud of you, and I know your father would be too. Robert would have been so thrilled to see you standing up for what you believe in."

Natalia's eyes filled with tears as she returned the embrace. "I need to get back. I promised Zath I'd return, and I don't want to worry him."

"I understand." Rosalie released her. "Be safe and tell your mate I look forward to meeting him." Her tone suggested she wasn't exactly anticipating it, but she was resigning herself to the idea.

"I will." Natalia turned and headed for the exit, her heart lighter than it had been in years. She had her mother's support, and she was hopeful for the future.

As she stepped out into the cool morning air, she breathed in the fresh scent of the flowers blooming nearby. The sun was rising over the horizon, painting the sky in shades of pink and orange. It was a beautiful sight, and she realized the world was healing, just like them.

She smiled, her heart full of joy. She was finally where she belonged, and she couldn't wait to share the news with Zath.

He was waiting for her in the lobby when she arrived back at the Embassy, his expression concerned. "I was worried about you, *vrash*. I knew you'd return, but I still worried."

"I'm sorry. I didn't mean to concern you." She wrapped her arms around him, breathing in his familiar scent. "I missed you."

"I missed you too." He nuzzled her neck, his tongue flicking out to taste her skin. "Did you speak with your mother?"

"I did." She leaned into his embrace, enjoying the warmth of his body. "She's willing to meet with you, but she's skeptical."

"I understand. I would be too." He cupped her cheek, gazing into her eyes. "Thank you. You don't know how much this means to me."

"I think I do." She smiled, her heart swelling with emotion. "I'm glad I can bring you two together. It's important to me."

"It's important to me too. I want peace, and I believe your mother can help us achieve it." His eyes glowed with an inner light. "We *will* change the world, my love."

She smiled, her eyes misting. "I believe you."

He kissed her, his tongue tangling with hers before he pulled back with a groan. "I want you."

She smiled. "Do you have time for a little afternoon delight, as they say?"

"Always." Practically at a run, he led her through the Embassy to their quarters, where he stripped her naked and laid her on the bed in record time.

"Mmm, you're overdressed." She tugged at his uniform.

"I can fix that." He shed his clothes and joined her, kissing her hungrily. His tongue tangled with hers, and she moaned into the kiss. His hands roamed her body, caressing her curves.

She gasped as he cupped her breasts, his thumbs brushing her nipples into hard peaks. She flinched, super sensitive.

He pulled back with a frown. "Are you all right?"

She nodded, swallowing. "I'm fine. Just...sensitive."

"Hmm." He lowered his head, capturing a nipple in his mouth. He sucked gently, and she cried out, arching her back. He continued his ministrations, teasing her with his tongue and teeth.

Suddenly, he jerked upright. "Why?"

With a slow smile, she took his hand and placed it against her belly. "I think you know why."

"You're with child?" His eyes lit up, and he grinned. "That's wonderful, vrash."

"I think I am, yes." She smiled. "I haven't confirmed it, but I suspect I am."

"Then we must celebrate." He kissed her, his tongue tangling with hers. "I can't wait to tell everyone."

She laughed, her heart swelling with happiness. "After orgasms."

"After orgasms," he agreed as he slid a hand between her legs, stroking her clit.

She moaned, her hips bucking as he rubbed her sensitive bud. "Yes, Zath. Right there."

He chuckled, his fingers moving faster. "Like this, *vrash*?"

"Yes." She gripped the sheets, her body tensing as pleasure washed over her. "I'm close." She panted, her eyes closing as she surrendered to the sensations.

He increased the pressure, and she exploded, crying out as her orgasm crashed through her. Her pussy clenched around his fingers, and she shuddered with release.

He withdrew his fingers, licking them clean. He was so sexy and sweet in that moment that she wanted to give him more pleasure than she'd ever given him. "I'm ready for both..."

He froze, his eyes widening. "You mean...?"

"Yes. I want you to fuck me with both your cocks."

He growled, his eyes flashing with desire. "I will, *vrash*, but I want to taste you first."

"Mmm, I like the sound of that." She grinned, spreading her legs. "Taste away."

He bent his head, his tongue darting out to lick her wet folds. She moaned, her hips bucking as he explored her slick heat. He teased her clit, making her gasp.

"Oh, yes." She writhed against his mouth, her eyes closed as she lost herself in the sensation. "Just like that."

He hummed, his tongue flicking her sensitive nub. She cried out, her back arching as pleasure washed over her. It wasn't enough to fully satisfy her though. "More, Zath. I need more." She was panting, her body trembling with need.

"As you wish." He rose, positioning himself between her legs. "Ready?"

"Yes." She nodded, her gaze locking with his. "Take me."

He pressed the tips of his cocks against her entrance, and she gasped as he slowly pushed inside her. He was thick and hard, stretching her to the limit.

"So tight. So perfect." He groaned, his eyes glowing with desire.

She moaned, her body adjusting to the intrusion. "So big. I can't believe you fit."

"You were made to take my cocks, *vrash*. Made for me." He thrust deeper, and she gasped, her pussy clenching around him. For a second, her body seemed poised to reject all of him, but then something eased, and both his cocks filled her.

"Yes, Zath. More." She panted, her nails digging into his shoulders as he drove into her. It hurt and felt amazing at the same time.

"Mine. All mine." He growled, his eyes glowing with desire as he increased the pace.

"Yours." She moaned, her body responding to his. "Harder, Zath. Fuck me harder."

He complied, his hemipenes moving in sync as he pounded into her. She cried out, her body shuddering as she came. He followed a moment later, filling her with both his cocks as he roared in pleasure.

They collapsed in a tangle of limbs, spent and sated. She snuggled against him, breathing in his familiar scent. "That was incredible."

He chuckled, his arm wrapping around her. "You were incredible, *vrash*. Your pussy is so tight, and you took both my cocks so well."

She smiled, blushing. "I enjoyed it."

He kissed her forehead. "I'm glad. I always want to give you pleasure."

She gazed up at him, her heart swelling with love. "You do. Every day."

He pulled her close, his eyes glowing with affection. "I love you, and I'm glad you're here with me."

"I love you too, Zath." She rested her head on his chest, listening to the steady beat of his heart.

He stroked her hair, his touch soothing. "Sleep, my love. Recover so I can ravish you again in a short time."

"Mmm, okay." She closed her eyes, soon drifting off to sleep in his arms.

Chapter Six

TWO WEEKS LATER, HE sat beside his mate and across the table from her mother. Rosalie was a lovely older version of Natalia. It was no wonder Pate could barely look away from her.

Natalia leaned closer, whispering, "The Grand Admiral is looking at my mom the way you look at me."

Zath chuckled. "He is. I noticed that as soon as they met. She's beautiful, and he's clearly smitten."

"I'm surprised. I thought he was a cold fish."

"No, he's a passionate male. He just hides it well," he said, his eyes twinkling.

Natalia looked at her mother, whose cheeks were flushed. "She's not immune either. I think she likes him."

"I believe she does. I can smell her arousal."

"Eww, Zath. That's my mom." Natalia wrinkled her nose.

"Sorry, *vrash*. It's an instinctual thing." He shrugged.

"I know. It's just weird to think of your mom as a sexual being."

"I understand, but I assure you, she is. And so is the Grand Admiral." He flicked out his tongue. "Your mother's pheromones suggest she's still capable of carrying offspring."

Natalia gaped. "Seriously? You're telling me my mom is ovulating?"

"I believe so, yes."

"Oh, geez. I don't need to know that." She grimaced. "I guess it's good news for the rebellion if she and the Grand Admiral hook up. She could bear the next leader of the Faction."

"Perhaps, but I believe they would be a formidable pair regardless." He smiled. "They seem quite taken with each other."

"Yeah, they do." She watched as her mother and the Grand Admiral exchanged glances, their eyes glowing with mutual interest.

"We should start the meeting." He regretted the need to interrupt the flirtation with practical matters.

"I agree, but I'm not sure how productive it will be if they can't keep their gazes off each other." She grinned.

"We'll see." He raised his voice. "Shall we begin?"

The Grand Admiral and Rosalie reluctantly tore their gazes from each other and focused on the matter at hand.

"Thank you." Zath smiled. "Now, let's discuss the terms of the treaty."

"I think we should start with the issue of human breeding rights," said Rosalie.

"Of course." Zath nodded. "What are your concerns?"

"I'm concerned that the Faction will continue to abduct humans and force them to breed." Rosalie's tone was firm. "I want assurances that will stop."

"I understand your concern, but the Faction has a limited number of females, and we don't abduct them, Rosalie," said Pate in a gravelly tone. "We negotiated with your government for the right to claim a small percentage of the population."

"That doesn't make it any better. It's still forced breeding." Rosalie's eyes flashed with anger.

"I understand your perspective, but the Faction needs to survive, and this is the only way." Pate's gaze was unwavering. "I'm not saying it's ideal, but it's necessary."

Rosalie sighed. "There has to be another way."

"If you have a suggestion, I'm open to hearing it." Pate's gaze was challenging.

"I'm working on it." Rosalie's jaw set in a stubborn line.

"I see." Pate's expression was amused.

"I do have one idea." Natalia spoke up.

"What is it?" asked Zath.

"What if there was a way to allow the women to choose their mates?" She glanced at her mother. "Would you be open to that?"

"I'm not sure." Rosalie frowned. "How would that work?"

"I'm not sure yet, but it's worth exploring, isn't it?" Natalia met her mother's gaze. "We could create a system where the women could select their partners from a pool of eligible males."

"That might work." Rosalie nodded slowly. "I'll think about it."

Zath regarded Natalia with curiosity. "We have been forming pairs working on the basis of genetic compatibility that requires the least modification."

"Yes, but it's always the compatible male who gets to choose. The one of highest rank, right?" asked Rosalie.

"Correct." Pate inclined his head.

"So, what if the choice was reversed?" Rosalie suggested. "What if the female had the final say?"

"Interesting." Zath tapped his chin. "Go on."

"We could create a database of available males and allow the females to choose from those." Rosalie's eyes sparkled with excitement. "They could even meet in person and get to know each other before making a decision."

"The idea has merit." Zath nodded. "It could improve the chances of successful matches."

"Our numbers aren't so dire now either," said Pate, looking thoughtful. "There is more time for negotiating breeding arrangements."

"Or making true matches," said Natalia as she put her hand on Zath's.

"Exactly." Rosalie smiled. "And it would give the women a sense of control over their futures."

"I think it's a great idea." Natalia grinned. "Right now, only about seventy percent of women stay with their alien and offspring. An element of choice might lead to more permanent matches too."

"What will happen to the human population if we all interbreed?" Rosalie frowned.

"Our population is down too, Mom. A lot of people died in the invasion, and we do have fewer men than women. If it's a choice, not an obligation, I bet there will be a lot more voluntary pairings," she said. "Most importantly, it restores choice for everyone, no matter with whom they partner, or how they build their families."

"I suppose you're right." Rosalie sighed. "I just want humanity to survive, and I'm not sure this is the best way."

"I understand, but I think it's worth trying. We can't go on like this forever." Natalia reached out and took her mother's hand. "We have to find a way to coexist, and this could be a step in the right direction."

"I know, but it's a lot to take in." Rosalie's expression was conflicted as she glanced at the Grand Admiral. "I'll have to think about it."

"Thank you." Zath smiled. "We're eager to find a solution that benefits all our species."

"I appreciate that." Rosalie met his gaze, her expression softening. "I want peace for my daughter's sake."

"As do I." Zath's eyes glowed with warmth as he looked at his mate. How he loved her.

Pate cleared his throat. "Let's adjourn for the evening. We can resume our discussions in the morning."

"Agreed." Zath stood, offering his hand to Natalia. "Shall we retire, *vrash*?"

"I'd love to."

As Zath took Natalia's hand, Pate asked, "May I take you to dinner, Rosalie?"

Rosalie blushed. "I'd like that."

Pate escorted her out, leaving Natalia and Zath alone.

"I think they're attracted to each other." Natalia looked amused.

"I think so too. It's a good sign." Zath smiled. "Your mother is a strong female."

"She is, but she's also lonely. My father's death hit her hard." Natalia's expression was thoughtful. "I think she's ready to move on."

"I hope so. They could be a powerful couple." Zath's eyes gleamed.

"I'm optimistic." Natalia smiled. "My mom deserves happiness."

"As do you, *vrash*." Zath's expression softened. "You've brought such joy to my life, and I can't imagine a world without you."

"Me neither." Natalia hugged him. "I love you, Zath."

"I love you too." He held her close, breathing in her scent. "I'm glad you're here with me."

"So am I." She smiled, her eyes shining with happiness.

"Come, let's go to bed." He led her to their bedroom, where he undressed her and tucked her into bed.

"I like this." She grinned, watching him remove his own clothes. It sent a pleasant shiver down his spine.

"I'm glad." He joined her in bed, pulling her into his arms. "I want to make you happy."

"You do." She snuggled against him, her skin warm and smooth. The feel of her body against his was intoxicating, and he couldn't resist the urge to explore. His hands roamed her curves, caressing her breasts and hips.

"Mmm, that feels nice." She arched into his touch, her eyes half-closed with pleasure.

"I'm glad." He smiled, his eyes glowing with desire. "You're so beautiful like this. So responsive."

"I can't help it. You make me feel so good." She sighed, her body relaxing under his ministrations.

"I want to make you feel even better." He bent his head to kiss her, recognizing the signs of exhaustion in her posture. "After you rest. I love you, *vrash*."

"I love you too." She yawned, her eyes closing.

He held her as she drifted off to sleep, his heart full of love. He was the luckiest male in the universe, and he would do whatever it took to keep her safe and happy.

Epilogue

SEVERAL MONTHS LATER, Natalia leaned against Zath, letting him support her aching back as her mother and Pate undertook the binding ceremony.

Theirs was one of the first under the new system that put the choice in the women's hands. It was a small gathering, but Rosalie and Pate seemed pleased.

Natalia was thrilled to see her mother happy again. After the loss of her father and the years of fighting the Faction, Rosalie deserved some peace.

Zath nuzzled her neck, his breath tickling her ear. "Are you ready to go home, vrash?"

"Yes, please." She smiled up at him, her heart full of love. "I'm ready for some quiet time with you." She was tired and sore from the long day, but it was worth it to see her mother mated to the Grand Admiral.

"I'll take care of you." He wrapped his arms around her, supporting her as they left the temple.

"I know you will." She relaxed in his embrace, trusting him to protect her. As they returned to their quarters, her abdomen tightened again. This time, she wasn't able to hide it from her mate as she'd done for most of the day, refusing to miss her mother's ceremony. She winced, her hand going to her stomach.

"What's wrong, *vrash*?" His eyes narrowed with concern. "Is it the babies?"

"I don't know." She tried to smile. "It's probably nothing."

"We should get you to the medical facility."

"No, it's fine." She shook her head. "I'm sure it's just Braxton Hicks contractions."

"Braxton Hicks?" He frowned. "What is that?"

"It's false labor. My body's getting ready for the babies." She rubbed her belly. "It's normal."

"If you're sure…"

"I still have two weeks…" She trailed off, wincing at the speed and intensity of the next contraction. It shouldn't be coming so regularly or intensely if it was false labor. "Or maybe not."

Zath scooped her up and carried her to the medical facility, shouting for assistance. He was panicked, and she was touched by his concern.

"I'm okay. It's okay." She patted his chest, trying to reassure him.

"You're in pain, and I don't like it." He scowled.

"I'm okay, really. It's normal." She smiled, her heart warmed by his concern. "I promise."

"If you say so." He didn't sound convinced.

"I do." She leaned up and kissed his cheek. "Trust me, Zath. I know my body, and I'm fine."

"All right, *vrash*." He nodded, but he kept his arm around her as Quillen joined them.

"Hello, Natalia." The doctor smiled. "I heard you were here. Is everything all right?"

"I'm fine." She smiled. "I think the babies are coming."

"Ah, yes. Let's take a look." The doctor scanned her belly with his scanner. "Hmm, you're right. It looks like you're in active labor. Your cervix is dilated, and you're effaced. I'd say you're about six centimeters."

"She's not due for two weeks. Keep them in," said Zath.

Quillen looked stunned as she giggled. "Earlier labor is quite common with twins, General, especially since your babies are larger than a human infant. There's no keeping them in now."

"What can you do?" Zath demanded.

"I can offer her medication for the pain, and I can assist with the delivery, but that's about it. She's fully dilated, and the babies are ready to come out." Quillen gave her a sympathetic smile. "It's too late to stop it."

"I can handle it." Natalia smiled, trying to reassure her mate. "It's okay, Zath. I'm ready to meet our children."

"I'm not." He looked pale, and she realized he was terrified.

She squeezed his hand. "It's going to be okay. I promise."

"I don't want you in pain." He cursed, a sibilant sound that echoed around the room. "This is my fault."

She couldn't help laughing. "I knew the risks, Zath. I chose this."

"Still, I should have—"

"Stop." She placed a finger over his lips. "I'm fine. The babies are fine. Everything is fine."

"I love you, Natalia." He kissed her forehead. "I don't want you to suffer."

"I love you too, Zath." Another contraction hit, and she gritted her teeth.

"I hate seeing you in pain." He stroked her hair, his eyes filled with worry.

"I'm okay." She smiled through the discomfort. "I promise."

"I believe you." He kissed her forehead. "I trust you, vrash."

"Good. Now, let's meet these babies." She grinned, her heart swelling with love even as pain rippled through her.

"I can't wait." His eyes glowed green in his excitement.

"Neither can I." She smiled, blinking back tears. As Quillen assisted with the delivery, Natalia pushed with all her might, bringing their first child into the world less than an hour later.

"Girl number-one, as expected." The doctor held up the squalling infant, and Zath cut the cord.

"She's beautiful." Natalia gazed at her daughter with awe. Genetically, she was mostly Serpentine, with a few human features. Her skin was a lovely shade of green, and her scales were a darker hue. She had a shock of dark hair and a tiny nose.

"She's perfect." Zath's voice was thick with emotion. "I love you, Natalia."

"I love you…" She trailed off as the baby opened her eyes, revealing luminous yellow irises.

"What's wrong?" Zath asked.

"Nothing." She blinked back tears. "She has color in her eyes all the time apparently. I guess I'm just humbled to see parts of me in her." How did proxies ever walk away from their babies?

"She's perfect, and so are you."

As another contraction hit a few minutes later, Natalia bore down, pushing with all her might.

"Here comes the second little girl." Quillen sounded reassuring.

"I see the head." Zath sounded awed.

"Push, Natalia." Quillen guided the baby's shoulders.

Natalia grunted, straining as the second child emerged. With a heavy exhalation, she laid back, exhausted, as the baby cried.

"Another girl, as anticipated. Genetic scans can't be wrong," said Quillen as Zath cut the cord, his eyes shining with pride. "This one is bigger than her sister."

"I believe it," she said with a tired smile as the nurse brought her second daughter closer.

They weren't identical. This baby had shimmering red skin and scales, and a mop of dark red hair. She also had the same yellow eyes as her sister but no nose. Just little slits like Zath's.

"My two girls." She felt overwhelmed with love and gratitude.

"You did well, *vrash*."

"Thanks." She smiled at her mate as the nurses cleaned the infants and swaddled them.

"What are their names?" asked Quillen as he held a datapad after helping her finish the delivery.

"Zaria after my mother," said Zath.

"And Robin after my father," said Natalia.

"Lovely names, but which girl is which?" asked the Med Chief.

She looked at Zath. "Do you want to choose?"

"I believe the elder should be Zaria, and the younger should be Robin." He smiled.

"Perfect." She nodded, her heart full of love. "That's what I was thinking too."

"I'm glad we agree." He kissed her forehead.

As the nurses handed her the babies, a wave of fierce protectiveness washed over her. "I can't believe they're ours."

"I can't believe we made them." He chuckled as he put his arms around all of them. "You were incredible, *vrash*."

"So were you." She smiled, gazing at their daughters. "I can't believe how much I love them already."

"I know." He kissed her forehead. "I love you, Natalia."

"I love you too, Zath." She smiled, her heart full of joy. This was the future she'd never expected, but she wouldn't change a thing. They were a family, and she was right where she belonged, in her place, at his side.

About Juno

JUNO WELLS GREW UP on Florida's Space Coast, watching the shuttles take off from Cape Canaveral. When she hit college, her childhood fantasies about space travel turned highly romantic. Now her mind reels with space adventures of fantastic alien lords in distant galaxies, and the earth women they love.

Wells' stories explore the complex, sensual relationships between inhabitants of different star systems. There are always happy endings just as there is always a new world to explore.

Have a comment? Make first contact with Juno at authorjunowells@gmail.com.

About Aurelia

AURELIA SKYE IS THE pen name *USA Today* Bestselling author Kit Tunstall uses when writing science fiction romance, paranormal romance, and paranormal women's fiction. It's simply a way to separate the myriad types of stories she writes so readers know what to expect with each "author."

<u>Website</u>[1]

---

1. http://www.kittunstall.com

Did you love *Baby For The Serp General*? Then you should read *Baby For The Grimlock General* by Aurelia Skye and Juno Wells!

She's been drafted to be a surrogate for the alien.

Violet Jones discovers she's been matched to a Grimlock general. She'll accompany the huge alien general to his home world. She only has to give him a year to woo her and act as his surrogate before she can walk away. At first, she's sure she can't give the massive alien what he wants, but he's completely contrary to what she expects. He's tender, caring, and obsessed with ensuring her pleasure and ability to accommodate him. Soon enough, the idea of leaving him seems crazier than the possibility of staying.

Seven years ago, the Faction agreed to save Earth from the Vorathan invasion in exchange for Earth women giving them one year of proxy rights to act as a surrogate, since the aliens of the Faction faced a dwindling population. With the Vorathans feared

throughout the galaxy as bloodthirsty, vicious marauders, the Earth's government agreed.

That doesn't mean the women did.

Sometimes, you want to read about the entire alien empire and all its myriad twists and turns, immersing yourself in hundreds of pages of intrigue. And sometimes, you want to skip the frills and get to the main event. Juno and Aurelia are pleased to bring you a series of short, steamy romances about untouched human women making babies with their truly alien mates.